A YEAR THROUGH MY EYES

a collection of poetry

Charles F. McDonald

Inkwell Publishing

Inkwell Publishing

This book is dedicated to the person who has always been by my side.

To my lovely wife,
For giving me the courage to write and sharing in every step of the way
With you by my side,
poetry is forever free

love charlie

INTRODUCTION

During the course of 2020 i chose to write down my thoughts throughout the year. I am a Scottish man born and breed but i lived the majority of my life in South Africa. When i moved to Sweden to live with my girlfriend it was a difficult change for me and i found that writing down my thoughts was the best expression of how i was feeling and observations of the world and people around me.

So, please follow along with the highs and lows of my year.

SPRING

"You can cut all the flowers but you cannot keep Spring from coming."

- Pablo Neruda

CHARLES MCDONALD

Bird song

As the sun starts to peek over the horizon,
the birds begin to sing.

Their cheerful tunes fill the air,
welcoming in a new day.

The birdsong is a symphony,
a beautiful melody.

It's a sign that nature is alive and well,
and that the world is a beautiful place.

Spring

The world is in bloom,
Nature is putting on a show,
The colours are so bright,
And the air is so fresh,

This is the time of year,
When new life is born,
Everything is so alive,
And there is so much hope,

So, let's celebrate,
This most wonderful season,
And all the joy it brings.

CHARLES MCDONALD

Country meadow

A field of flowers,
Is a beautiful sight
To see,

A meadow of flowers,
Is a peaceful place
To be,

You can smell the fragrance
Of the flowers in the air,
And feel the warm sun
On your face,

The flowers are nodding
In the gentle breeze,
And the butterflies
Are fluttering by,

It's a tranquil scene,
And it fills your heart
With joy

The winds of spring

The warm breeze flutters,
The leaves on the trees,
The sun shines down,
And the world is at peace

The birds are singing,
And the bees are buzzing,
The flowers are blooming,
And all is right with the world

For just a moment,
All is calm and serene,
And we can breathe in,
The beauty of nature

But soon enough,
The wind will pick up,
The clouds will roll in,
And the world will be as it was

But for now, we enjoy,
The peace of the warm breeze

CHARLES MCDONALD

Butterflies

Blurring by in a flurry of colour,
Unbelievable beauty on fragile wings,
Gentle flapping in a nonchalant way,
Butterflies bring a smile to my face

They are nature's little wonders,
Incredibly intricate and lovely,
A joy to behold on a summer day

These fragile creatures are amazing,
Their short life full of flitting and fluttering,
A reminder to enjoy the simple things

Butterflies are a magical thing,
They can take my worries away,
With their beauty and grace

For a little while, I can forget,
And just enjoy the moment

When life is moving too fast,
And I need a reminder to slow down,
I watch the butterflies and remember

How to simply enjoy life.

The forgotten frost

Spring is a time of rebirth,
When the earth comes alive again,
The trees bud and the flowers bloom,
The air is filled with the scent of life,
The world is new again,

Life is everywhere, in the cells of the trees,
And in the silent pulsing of the rain,
In the voice of the bird crying in the night,
And in the endless mystery of the stars,
Spring is a time of hope,

When the bleakness of winter is forgotten,
And the promise of summer fills the air,
It's a time to start anew,
To plant the seeds of our dreams,
And watch them grow It's a time of wonder,

When the world is alive with new possibilities,
So let's embrace the change as an old friend,
And all the hope and life it brings,
Welcome its arrival with open hearts,
And let its beauty fill our hearts and minds.

CHARLES MCDONALD

Rebirth

The world is new again,
After the long, dark winter.

The sun is shining,
The birds are singing,
And the flowers are blooming.

It's a time for new beginnings,
For hope and happiness.

Let's make the most of this fresh start,

And create a bright future.

That special day

It's time to celebrate
Two hearts joining as one
All our family and friends
Gathered together to have some fun
We'll dance and laugh and toast
And wish the happy couple all the best
They'll start their life together
With love in their hearts and smiles on their faces
We'll all be there to support them
Every step of the way
As they begin their journey

Down the aisle of life

CHARLES MCDONALD

Nordic spring

When the snow melts away
And the sun shines bright
There's a feeling in the air
That can only be described as spring

The flowers start to bloom
The birds start to sing
And everyone feels a little bit lighter
A little bit happier

When spring comes to Sweden
The whole country feels alive
And we can't help but smile

So let's enjoy this time
Of warmer days and longer nights
And cherish every moment
Of this Swedish spring

Morning fika

It's time for fika,
my favourite time of day.
When we all gather round
and enjoy each other's company.

There's nothing quite like it,
a chance to sit and chat
and catch up on all the news.

And of course, the food is lovely too.
You can't beat a good fika
for making you feel happy and content.

CHARLES MCDONALD

House by the lake

I long for a lake house
where I can just be
and enjoy the simple things
in life once again.

I miss the sound of the water
lapping against the shore
and the smell of the pine trees
in the air.

I can't wait to feel
the warm sun on my face
and breathe in the fresh air
of the countryside.

I'm ready to relax

and escape the hustle and bustle
of everyday life.
I can't wait to be
surrounded by nature

and recharge my soul.

Easter

A little chocolate here,
a little chocolate there.
Some people like it dark,
some people like it white.
I like my chocolate
in between.

It's not too sweet,
it's not too rich.
The perfect balance
of flavour and texture.

And on Easter Sunday,
when the chocolate is plentiful,
I indulge in my favourite treat.

I may not be religious,
but I bow down
to the power of Easter chocolate.

CHARLES MCDONALD

Thinking of home

The misty rolling hills,
The deep blue lochs and trees,
The heather on the moors,
The sound of bagpipes in the air,

These are the things that make Scotland so special to me.

It's a land of great beauty and history,
And a place that I'm proud to be from.

When I'm feeling homesick or down,
All I have to do is close my eyes,
And I can picture the bonnie Scotland,
That i love so much.

That day in January

Oh haggis, oh haggis
The pride of Scottish cuisine
My favourite traditional dish
I savour every bite of you
Your sheep heart, liver and lungs
Minced with oatmeal, onions, and spices
So succulent, so savoury
I can't get enough of you
And I'm not the only one
For haggis is beloved by many
A national dish of Scotland
And the perfect comfort food
So, if you're ever feeling blue
Just have some haggis

And you'll be sure to feel better

CHARLES MCDONALD

The start of the end

As the days grow hotter,
the air grows thick and sticky.
The sun beats down relentlessly,
and the pavement seems to shimmer.

There's a hazy haze in the air,
and the trees droop in the heat.
The grass is brown and crispy,
and the flowers are drooping.

But despite the heat and the humidity,
there's still a beauty in the summer days.
The colours are brighter,
and the days are longer.

So enjoy the summertime,
even though it might be hot.
because before you know it,
it will be gone.

Evergreen

Floating on a gentle breeze
Trees swaying back and forth
Leaves rustle and whisper
A cool wind in the summer heat
The leaves are so green
They look like they're glowing
The trees are so tall
They seem to touch the sky
I can't help but wonder
How much beauty there is

In the world around me.

CHARLES MCDONALD

First swim

The first swim of the year is always such a treat,
Especially after a long winter when we're feeling beat.

We can't wait to get in, the water is so revitalizing,
And we forget all about the cold weather outside.

Swimming is such a great way to get some exercise,
And it's also a lot of fun, so it's no surprise

That the first swim of the year is always so exciting,

Can't wait to do it again, hope the weather
keeps cooperating!

Just breathe

taking a breath is like taking in the world
it's like feeling the air fill your lungs
and letting it out slowly
it's like hearing the sound of the world

and feeling the peace that comes with it

CHARLES MCDONALD

Finding my quiet

I sit under the tree
and let the words flow out of me
They come easily in the quiet
and I am at peace

The sun filters through the leaves
and the breeze is a gentle caress
I am in my element
and the world is at my feet

This is my happy place
where I can lose myself
in the act of creation

It is a place of refuge
where I can go to escape
the demands of life

And for a little while
I am the only one that matters

The world fades away
and I am lost in the beauty

of the words that flow from me

Unknown

The places we used to go
Are now becoming something new
The things we used to know
Are now being rearranged
It's hard to keep up with the changes
But we must go with the flow
And see where the new landscape takes us
Who knows what we'll find
But it's sure to be an adventure
So let's go explore

And see what this new world has in store

SUMMER

"In early June the world of leaf and blade and flowers explode, and every sunset is different."

- John Steinbeck

The welcome rain

It's starting to rain
The summer rain is falling
The drops are getting bigger
And the thunder is growling
The lightning is flashing
The wind is picking up
And the rain is coming down
The waves are crashing
The sun is shining
And the rain is pouring
The clouds are dark
And the sky is gray
The temperature is dropping
And the rain is getting heavy
The wind is blowing
And the rain is pelting
The trees are swaying
And the branches are breaking
The power is out
And the lights are flickering
The rain is coming down in sheets
And the floodwaters are rising
The roads are washed out
And the bridges are collapsing
The levees are breaking
And the levees are failing
The water is everywhere

And the summer rain is falling

CHARLES MCDONALD

Harvest

A farms harvest is a time of great excitement
The farmers are busy in the field
The animals are busy in the barn
The workers are busy in the kitchen
All preparing for the big day

The fields are full of colour
The air is full of the scent of fresh food
The sky is full of the sound of laughter

All the hard work of the season comes to this one moment
When the fruits of the farm are gathered in

And everyone enjoys the bounty of the harvest

A place by the sea

The sea is a mysterious place,
A place where creatures great and small
Make their homes.

And when I swim in its depths,
I feel like I am a part of something
Much larger than myself.

The water is cool and refreshing,
And the movement of the waves
Is soothing and hypnotic.

I can lose myself for hours in the sea,
And when I come up for air,

I feel like I have been reborn.

Billowing

The clouds are building up
Slowly but surely
Piled high in the sky
A mass of grey and white
A storm is brewing
The wind is picking up
The air is thick with anticipation
The sky is darkening
The first few drops of rain begin to fall

The storm is here

Serenity

The big oak tree stands tall and strong

With branches reaching up to the sky
Its leaves rustle in the breeze
And birds nest in its branches
The big oak tree is a sight to behold
And it's a wonderful place to play
Hide and seek, or just sit and dream
The big oak tree is a friend to all

And it will be here for years to come

CHARLES MCDONALD

A Simple Joy

When the pizza's in the oven
And the room starts to heat
The smell of cheese and tomato
Makes my mouth start to water
I can't wait to take a bite
Of that fresh, hot pizza
I hope it's nice and gooey
With a crispy crust
I'll eat it with my fingers
And licking my lips
I'll savour every flavour

Till the last crumb is gone

Strawberry

I know strawberries,
I've seen them grow
I've seen them in the store
I've seen them on the plate

I know strawberries,
I've picked them myself
I've eaten them fresh
I've made them into jam

I know strawberries,
Sweet and sour and red
A burst of flavor in my mouth
Every time that I eat them

I know strawberries,
And I love them so
In the summertime or winter
Whenever they are in season

I know strawberries,
And I'm so glad I do

For they are one of nature's treasures

CHARLES MCDONALD

Farmyard

    The animals on the farm
    Are so full of love and charm
    They make the perfect friends
    And they're always there to help
    You with whatever you need
    They're always there to lend a hand
    And they're always ready to play
    No matter what the hour
    The animals on the farm

    Are the best friends you could ever have

Summer days

Laying under the sun
On a hot summer's day
My skin starts to feel the heat
And I'm starting to sweat

I close my eyes and enjoy
The warmth on my face
I can feel my body relax

As I drift off to sleep

CHARLES MCDONALD

The feast

When the days are longest
And the sun is hottest
We celebrate the summer
With feasting and fun
The night is short
But the memories last
For all of us to cherish

Until the next midsummer

Freshly mown grass

The sun is beating down,
And the sweat is pouring.
I grab the trusty lawnmower,
And get to work mowing.

The grass is already so high,
That it's almost to my knee.
But I keep on going,
To make it look nice and neat.

The fumes from the mower,
Are making me feel lightheaded.
But I carry on working,
Until the job is done.

Then I can sit back,
And survey my handy work.
The lawn looks so much better,

Now that it's been cut.

CHARLES MCDONALD

Seasons change

When the leaves start to turn
And the air gets chilly
We know that autumn is here
Bringing with it joy and cheer

The days are shorter now
But we don't mind
We can still enjoy the beauty
Of this wonderful time

Everything looks so different
In the autumn light
And we can't help but smile
As we take in the sight

So let's enjoy this season
And all that it brings
For before we know it

Winter will be here

Self-motivation

The sun is up, the sky is blue
There's not a cloud to be seen
The perfect day for doing what you want to do
So get up and make the most of it

There's nothing better than a day in the sun
Especially when it's shining just for you
So make the most of every moment
And enjoy the warmth and the light

For soon enough it will be gone
And you'll be left longing for more
So make the most of every sunny day

And enjoy the sunshine while it lasts

Do you want to go for a walk?

Walking my dog is one of my favourite things to do
It brings me so much joy and happiness
My dog loves it too, she gets to sniff and explore
And chase any squirrels that she might see

Walking with my dog is a great way to start the day
It gets me moving and helps me to clear my head
And my dog is always so happy and excited
To be outside and spending time with me

I cherish our walks together, they are a highlight of my day
And I know that no matter what else happens

We will always have our walks to look forward to

The feeling of summer

The sand is warm and gritty
Between my toes
I feel the beach's presence
With each step I take
The sound of waves crashing
Fills my ears
And the smell of salt water
Is like a tonic
This is my happy place
Where I can feel the sand

Between my toes

It sounds like

The music of summertime
is the sound of happiness
the sound of laughter
the sound of life

It's the sound of ice cubes
clinking in glasses
the sound of waves
crashing on the shore

The music of summertime
is the sound of memories
being made

It's the sound of friends
talking and joking
the sound of kids
playing and having fun

The music of summertime
is the sound of love
It's the sound of hearts
beating as one

The music of summertime
is the sound of happiness
the sound of laughter

Crystal blue

The sound of the water
dripping and splashing
echoing through the room
filling the air with its cool freshness.

The feel of the water
running over my skin
as I dip my toes in
and let out a sigh.

The smell of the water
clean and pure
inviting me to dive in
and forget everything else.

The taste of the water
chilly and refreshing
quenching my thirst
and making me feel alive.

The sight of the water
sparkling in the sun
as it cascades down
a mountain of rocks.

This is the water
that I need
that I can't live without.

CHARLES MCDONALD

Summer treat

There's nothing quite like a scoop of ice cream
On a hot summer day
It melts in your mouth
And cools you right down

There are so many flavours
To choose from
So many colours
And textures

But no matter which one you choose
They're all delicious
And they all hit the spot

Ice cream is the perfect treat
For young and old alike
It's a classic for a reason

So next time you're feeling hot and sticky
Grab a cone or a bowl

And enjoy a little bit of summer heaven

Fresh air

The fresh air is invigorating
And the sun is so bright
I can barely keep my eyes open
As I try to read my book.

The pages are flying by
As the story unfolds
I can't wait to see what happens next

This is the best way to spend my day
Lost in a good book
obtaining new knowledge
And enjoying nature's way.

CHARLES MCDONALD

Slumber

Sleepy me,
Sleeping in a hammock
Swaying back and forth
Gentle breeze
 Rustling leaves
Rock me to sleep
Dreaming of faraway places

Wondering what tomorrow will bring

AUTUMN

"And all the lives we ever lived and all the lives to be are full of trees and changing leaves."

- Virginia Woolf

CHARLES MCDONALD

Roar of the fire

The fire roars in the fireplace
The flames are high and bright
The heat is intense and warm
The wood is crackling and burning
The smoke is rising and swirling
The room is filled with the glow
The fire is roaring and alive
It's a beautiful sight to see
The fire is crackling and burning
The wood is crackling and burning
The flames are high and bright
The room is filled with the glow
The heat is intense and warm
The smoke is rising and swirling
It's a beautiful sight to see
The fire is roaring and alive

In a passed life

The old farm barn
Is falling down
The roof is caving in
The walls are crumbling
The windowpanes are shattered
The door is hanging off its hinges

But still, it stands
A testament to a bygone era
When farming was a way of life
And the barn was the heart of the farm

Now it is empty and forgotten
But it still stands tall and proud
A reminder of a time when things were simpler

And the world was a different place

CHARLES MCDONALD

In the country

The hills roll gently, like a great green wave
that crests and falls and rises again.
In between are hidden valleys,
and alpine meadows full of wildflowers.

The air is clean and crisp,
with the scent of pine and fir trees.
And in the distance, always,
are the snow-capped mountains,
majestic and enduring.

This is the Swedish landscape,
a land of great beauty and peace.
It calls to the heart and soul,

welcoming all who come.

Endless nights

Summer is drawing to a close
And the days are getting shorter
But the nights, ah the nights
They just keep getting longer

The air is thick with humidity
And the stars are hidden away
But the darkness, it just keeps creeping in
Slowly, steadily, until it's here to stay

The fireflies have all died out
And the crickets have gone quiet
But the night, it just drones on

With no end in sight

CHARLES MCDONALD

My perfect meal

Sugar and spice and everything nice
that's what apple pies are made of

There's nothing quite like a warm slice
of apple pie, served with a dollop
of whipped cream on top

The flaky crust, the sweet filling
is what makes this dessert so heavenly

When cold weather hits, there's nothing
That warms you up quite like warm apple pie

So next time you're feeling chilly,
just take a bite of this tasty treat

And all your troubles will melt away

Gamla Stan

The old town is a place of history

A place where the past is still alive

You can feel it in the air

As you walk through the streets

The old town is a place of beauty

A place where the present is still alive

You can see it in the buildings

As you walk through the streets

The old town is a place of memories

A place where the future is still alive

You can dream it in your mind

As you walk through the streets

CHARLES MCDONALD

Rain by night

It's a cold night
the rain is pouring down
but inside its cosy and dry
the candles are flickering
and the fire is warm
its a perfect night to stay in
with a good book and a cup of tea
the world outside can wait
tonight is for relaxing

and enjoying the peace and quiet

In the forest

The woods are a magical place
Where the trees are so tall
And the sunbeam filters through
It's a place where I can be free
And just breathe

I love to take a walk in the woods
And feel the crunch of the leaves
And smell the fresh air
It's like a piece of heaven
And it's a place where I feel most alive

There's something about the woods
That just makes me feel good
And I can't help but smile
When I'm walking in nature's beauty

It's a place to reflect and dream
And to just be in the moment
It's a place to feel connected
To the earth and all of its wonder

So take a walk in the woods
And let nature surround you
And let the peace of the woods

Settle into your soul

CHARLES MCDONALD

Chestnuts roasting over an open fire

When I was younger
and my nose was colder
I would love to roast chestnuts
over an open fire

The smell of burning wood
and the sound of cracking nuts
would make my heart sing

Now, even though I'm older
and my nose is not quite so cold
I still love to roast chestnuts
over an open fire

The smell of burning wood
and the sound of cracking nuts

still make my heart sing

Lost

There's something thrilling about getting lost
In the moment you realize you have no clue
Where you are, or how to get back
The panic sets in and your heart starts to race
You start to sweat, and your mind starts to race
As you search for some way out
The way you came in seems like a stranger
You're lost in the moment and it's exciting
Even though you know you should be scared
You can't help but to be thrilled

By the adventure of getting lost

Shimmering green

The northern lights

are a beautiful sight

They are like a rainbow

in the night

And when you see them

you can't help but smile

They are just so amazing

And always make me feel so happy

I could stare at them forever

And never get bored

I always feel so lucky

When I get to see the northern lights

Change

The air is crisp and the sky is blue

The leaves are starting to turn

It's time to go apple picking

We head to the farm

And fill our baskets with apples

Red, green, and yellow

We eat a few as we pick

And the kids get sticky faces

It's a perfect day

For apple picking

CHARLES MCDONALD

Good morning

Strong and black
the coffee hits my system
jolting me awake
after a long night.

I sit at the kitchen table
wrapped in a comfy blanket
cool morning air
nipping at my nose.

With a book in my hands
and a cat on my lap
I slowly sip my coffee
as the world around me

begins to wake up.

In the morning

I walk to work each morning,
my feet dragging along the pavement.
I'm not looking forward to another day
of boredom and mediocrity.

I'd much rather be curled up in bed,
lost in a book or sleeping.

But instead I trudge along,
wishing I could find a better way.

I'm counting down the days
until I can retire and finally
be free from this daily grind.

Until then,
I'll just keep on walking,

one foot in front of the other.

WINTER

"Winter, a lingering season, is a time to gather golden moments, embark upon a sentimental journey, and enjoy every idle hour."

- John Boswell

Flakes of snow

The first snow is always so magical
Everything is so quiet and still
The world is blanketed in white
And it's so beautiful to behold

I can't help but feel happiness
When I see the snow falling down
It's like the world is brand new
And everything is possible

The first snow is a time to cherish
A time to be with loved ones
And to create lasting memories

That will be cherished forever

Standing alone

The summer house stands empty now,

Its windows dark, its door half-open.
The grass is long around it, weeds
Entwine the porch where once we sat.

Time has passed since we were here,
Since laughter echoed in these rooms,
Since we picnicked on the lawn
And watched the fireflies at night.

The summer house is just a shell,
But memories live on of happy times,
Of family and friends gathered round,

Of warm days and starry nights.

The spirit of Christmas

Christmas is a time for giving
And a time for being with family
It's a time for happiness and love
And for making cherished memories

Christmas is a time for laughter
And for sharing stories and smiles
It's a special time of year
And one that we always hold dear

So whatever this holiday season brings
Whether it's joy or sorrow or cheer
We'll cherish each moment
And the memories we make

For Christmas is a time for everything

And it's a time that we always hold dear

CHARLES MCDONALD

New beginnings

As the clock strikes midnight
A new year has begun
A time to start anew
To leave the past behind

A time for resolutions
For hope and for dreams
To make them come true

So let's raise a glass
To the new year ahead
May it be filled with happiness

And all that you need

Snowball

When the snow is freshly fallen
And the air is still and cold,
We'll bundle up and head outside
For a snowball fight.

We'll build up walls of snow
To protect us from the onslaught,
And pelting each other with snowballs
Until we're covered head to toe.

It's so much fun to be a kid

And have a snowball fight.

Shovelling

The snow is falling gently down,
And I am stuck inside my house.
I look out the window and see
That my shovel is still in the same spot.

I bundle up in my coat and scarf,
And head out into the frigid air.
I know that I'll be cold,
But I also know that I'll feel better

Once I've gotten some exercise.
So, I trudge through the snow,
Shovel in hand,
And start the tedious task of shovelling.

It's not the most fun I've ever had,
But it's necessary, nonetheless.
And when I'm done,
I can go back inside

And enjoy the rest of my day,

Warm and safe and sound.

Family dinner

I can smell it even before I open the door
  garlic and spices wafting through the air
  it's time for family dinner once again

We all gather around the table
  eager to fill our plates
  with mom's homemade lasagna

There's always lots of laughs and smiles
  as we share stories from our day
  it's just what we need to recharge

And as we sit there content
  we're glad we can all be together

for another delicious family dinner

Skating the lake

The blade tip first kisses the ice
Then eases its way forward
In a fluid movement
The weightless body follows
Until it is spinning
And then end over end
Till it is a blur

The speed is exhilarating
The scenery a blur
All that matters is the next move
The next edge
The next jump
Till finally
The music slows
And the blades scrape to a stop

In the silence
We are surrounded by our own world
 Created by our movements
A place where only we exist
And for a moment

We are free

Twinkle, twinkle

> The twinkling lights
> They bring to life
> The memories of loved ones
> And the laughter of friends
> They shine so bright
> And lift our spirits high
> We can't help but feel
> Their warmth and love
>
> As they twinkle in the night

CHARLES MCDONALD

Christmas baking

Smelling of gingerbread,
spicy and sweet,
it fills the house with holiday cheer.

Baked with love and care,
to share with family and friends,
its aroma is impossible to resist.

Making mouths water,
stomachs grumble,

it's the smell of Christmas in the air.

Lookout point

From my perch atop the hill
I survey the scene below
The trees are laden with white
And the ground is covered in snow

The air is crisp and cold
And the sky is a deep blue
All around is so tranquil
And so very beautiful

The snowflakes are falling
And the icicles are shining
What a magical winter scene

That I am beholding

Leather gloves

The world is cold and my hands are bare

I need some gloves to keep them warm

There's no better feeling than when

I put on my winter gloves

And my hands are suddenly happy

They're toasty and comfortable

And I can go about my business

Without having to worry

About my poor fingers freezing

So thank you, winter gloves

For keeping my hands safe and sound

And making my winter days a little bit brighter

Family time

There's something about baking cookies
That just makes everything feel right
The world outside may be chaos
But in the kitchen, it's all calm

The dough is smooth beneath my fingers
As I crumble in the chocolate chips
I know that in a few short minutes
These cookies will be perfect

And when they come out of the oven
All golden and crispy and warm
I can't help but smile

Because baking cookies
Is one of the simplest joys in life

And it's something that I'll always love

Darkness comes

The cold crisp night

brings a chill to my bones

but I find comfort

in the blanket of stars

that wraps around me

like a cloak of protection.

I am not afraid

of the darkness

for I know the light

of the morning

will come again.

Steamy, sweaty and hot

The sauna, a place to detox

To sweat out all the toxins

To relax and feel the heat

To reflect on what's important

And let go of what's not.

That feeling

I love the feel of the cold water

I love the way it numbs my skin

I love the way it makes my body feel

I love the way it makes me feel alive

I love the way it makes me feel free

I love the way it makes me feel like I can do anything

I love the way it makes me feel like I belong

I love the way it makes me feel at home

THE END

Thank you for being apart of this journey.